# Best Friends

by Catherine Daly
illustrated by Tom Brannon

Simon Spotlight

New York    London    Toronto    Sydney    Singapore

Based on the TV series *Bear in the Big Blue House*™
created by Mitchell Kriegman. Produced by
The Jim Henson Company for Disney Channel.

Ojo was excited. She was expecting a special visitor. "Is Christine here yet?" she asked anxiously.

"You're really looking forward to Christine coming over, aren't you, Ojo?" asked Bear.

"Oh, yeah, Bear," replied Ojo. "Christine is one of my best friends!"

Bear smiled. "There's nothing like spending the day with a good friend!" he said. "Friends make everything fun."

*Dingdong,* rang the doorbell.

Ojo hopped up and down with excitement. "That must be her now!" she said. "Hurry, Bear! Hurry!"

Bear opened the front door. Ojo was right. It was Christine Rabbit.

"Hi, Christine!" exclaimed Ojo. "I've got all kinds of cool stuff that we can do today! We can draw with my crayons, play house . . ."

"Wow," said Bear. "That sounds like fun!"

Ojo and Christine hopped up and down. There were so many fun things for them to do together!

A little while later, Bear stepped into the living room. Ojo and Christine had spread blankets and pillows all over the floor.

"Are you pretending to camp out?" asked Bear.

Ojo and Christine shook their heads. "We're building a pillow castle. It's a lot of hard work!" said Ojo. Christine nodded.

Just then, Tutter came in. "Hi, Bear! Hi, Ojo! Hi, Christine! So who's up for a friendly game of checkers?"

Ojo smiled. "Thanks for asking, Tutter, but my best friend Christine and I are building a pillow castle. Do you want to help?"

Tutter's jaw dropped. "Best friend?" he said. "Christine is your *best friend*?"

"Um . . . well . . . ," said Ojo.

"Well, Ojo, you just go right ahead and play with your best friend Christine!" Tutter stomped out of the room.

Bear found Tutter sulking at the kitchen table.

"Are you okay?" Bear asked.

"Yes, Bear," said Tutter.

"Are you sure?" Bear asked.

"Sure I'm sure!" said Tutter. "If Ojo's busy with her best friend, well, that's fine, Bear. Just fine with me!"

*Roar!*

Bear stood up and walked to the kitchen door. "Hey!" he said. "It sounds like something's going on at the otter pond!"

Tutter sighed. "Go ahead, Bear," he said. "Don't you worry about me. No problems here!"

*Roar!*

"I'll be back as soon as I find out what's going on," said Bear.

Bear found Pip, Pop, and Treelo at the otter pond. Treelo was pretending to be a scary monster, and Pip and Pop didn't like it very much!

"Treelo, cut it out!" Pip and Pop said.

"What's the problem?" Bear wanted to know.

Everyone had a different story. Pip and Pop wanted to play their favorite game, Deep-Sea Divers, and didn't want to play Monster. Treelo wanted to play Monster and didn't want to play Deep-Sea Divers.

"Come on, you guys," said Bear. "I'm sure you can work this out."

Pip and Pop shook their heads. "If Treelo won't play our game then maybe he's not our . . . friend."

"Pip and Pop not my friend?" Treelo said sadly.

"Pip, Pop," Bear said, "you don't really think that's true, do you?"

"It's a shame you guys can't all work together as friends, because I know this really cool game called The Hidden Treasure of Kalamazoo Bay," said Bear. "You need two deep-sea divers and a pretend scary monster."

"How do you play? How do you play?" everyone asked.

"Well, the two divers come out of Kalamazoo Bay onto dry land, and suddenly, they run into a pretend scary monster!" Bear explained.

Everyone thought that sounded like a great game. Treelo hid and jumped out at the two divers. "Aaaaaah!" yelled Pip and Pop. "Good scary monster, Treelo," they said.

When Bear went back inside, he found Tutter sitting at the kitchen table playing checkers with a large piece of Swiss cheese. "What?" Tutter asked the cheese. "Oh, yes, that would be an excellent move. Thanks for the advice!"

"Um, Tutter, is everything okay?" Bear asked.

"Everything's great, Bear," said Tutter. "Meet my new best friend, Mr. Cheese! Mr. Cheese says I'm his best friend ever!"

Bear was puzzled. "Isn't that a piece of cheese?" he asked.

"Cheese has always been a good friend to this mouse," Tutter explained, "unlike a certain little girl bear cub named Ojo!"

"Tutter," began Bear, "I know that Ojo said Christine was her best friend, but I bet there's something you didn't know!"

"What?" said Tutter.

"You can have more than one best friend," Bear said.

"You can?" replied Tutter.

"Sure!" said Bear. "After all, you're my best friend, and so is Ojo, and Pip and Pop, and Treelo."

"Gee, I never thought of it like that before, Bear!" said Tutter.

"I bet Christine and Ojo would really like you to play with them," Bear said.

Tutter thought for a moment. "Okay, let's go!' he said.

In the living room, Ojo and Christine were still playing inside their pillow castle. They were setting the table for tea.

Tutter didn't want to bother them. "It sounds like they're busy," he said.

Bear had an idea. "Why don't you play near them and see what happens?"

Tutter walked over to the pillow castle and began to play. He pretended he had a beautiful garden right next to the castle. "I think I'll water my garden!" he said loudly. "Water, water, water, water."

Ojo and Christine heard Tutter and popped their heads out of the castle. "Hello, Tutter!" said Ojo. "Would you like to come inside and join us for tea?"

Tutter gasped. "Would I?" he said. "You really want me to?"

"Sure!" exclaimed Ojo. "Now I have two of my bestest friends to play with! Come on inside!"

"What a wonderful day," Bear said to himself that night. "I think I'll go upstairs and tell Luna all about it." Bear stepped out onto the balcony. And there was Luna, shining brightly.

"Hello, Luna!" he said.

"Hello, Bear!" replied Luna. "And how was your day at the Big Blue House?"

"It was great, Luna!" said Bear. "Christine Rabbit came over to play with Ojo. And Tutter joined them. And Pip, Pop, and Treelo all played The Treasure of Kalamazoo Bay."

Luna smiled. "I remember you playing that when you were a cub, Bear! You were quite a treasure hunter."

Bear chuckled. "Gee, you know me so well, Luna."

"Well, of course I do, Bear," said Luna. "We've been friends a long time. And friends know you better than anyone. Good night, Bear!"

Bear waved as Luna rose high in the night sky. "Good night, my friend!" he called to her.